¿Qué hay en el estanque, querido dragón?

What's in the Pond, Dear Dragon?

por/by Margaret Hillert

ilustrado por/Illustrated by David Schimmell

NORWOOD HOUSE PRESS

Queridos padres y maestros:

La serie para lectores principiantes es una colección de lecturas cuidadosamente escritas, muchas de las cuales ustedes recordarán de su propia infancia. Cada libro comprende palabras de uso frecuente en español e inglés y, a través de la repetición, le ofrece al niño la oportunidad de practicarlas. Los detalles adicionales de las ilustraciones refuerzan la historia y le brindan la oportunidad de ayudar a su niño a desarrollar el lenguaje oral y la comprensión.

Primero, léale el cuento al niño; después deje que él lea las palabras con las que está familiarizado y pronto, podrá leer solito todo el cuento. En cada paso, elogie el esfuerzo del niño para que se sienta más confiado como lector independiente. Hable sobre las ilustraciones y anime al niño a relacionar el cuento con su propia vida.

Sobre todo, la parte más importante de la experiencia de la lectura es ¡divertirse y disfrutarla!

Shannon Cannon

Shannon Cannon
Consultora de lectoescritura

Dear Caregiver,

The *Beginning-to-Read* series is a carefully written collection of readers, many of which you may remember from your own childhood. This book, *Dear Dragon's Day with Father*, was written over 30 years after the first *Dear Dragon* books were published. The *New Dear Dragon* series features the same elements of the earlier books, such as text comprised of common sight words. These sight words provide your child with ample practice reading the words that appear most frequently in written text. The many additional details in the pictures enhance the story and offer the opportunity for you to help your child expand oral language skills and develop comprehension.

Begin by reading the story to your child, followed by letting him or her read familiar words and soon your child will be able to read the story independently. At each step of the way, be sure to praise your reader's efforts to build his or her confidence as an independent reader. Discuss the pictures and encourage your child to make connections between the story and his or her own life.

Above all, the most important part of the reading experience is to have fun and enjoy it!

Shannon Cannon

Shannon Cannon,
Literacy Consultant

Norwood House Press • P.O. Box 316598 • Chicago, Illinois 60631
For more information about Norwood House Press please visit our website at *www.norwoodhousepress.com* or call 866-565-2900.
Text copyright ©2014 by Margaret Hillert. Illustrations and cover design copyright ©2014 by Norwood House Press, Inc. All rights reserved. No part of this book may be reproduced or utilized in any form or by any means without written permission from the publisher.
Designer: The Design Lab

LIBRARY OF CONGRESS CATALOGING-IN-PUBLICATION DATA

Hillert, Margaret.
  ¿Qué hay en el estanque, querido dragón?= What's in the pond, dear dragon? / por Margaret Hillert ; ilustrado por David Schimmell ; traducido por Queta Fernandez.
    pages cm. -- (A beginning-to-read book)
  Summary: "A boy and his pet dragon go exploring at a nearby pond. They learn about fish, plants, and boats that can be found in ponds. This title includes reading activities"-- Provided by publisher.
  ISBN 978-1-59953-608-8 (library edition : alk. paper) -- ISBN 978-1-60357-616-1 (ebook)
  [1. Ponds--Fiction. 2. Nature--Fiction. 3. Dragons--Fiction. 4. Spanish language materials--Bilingual.] I. Schimmell, David, illustrator. II. Fernandez, Queta, translator. III. Hillert, Margaret. ¿Qué hay en el estanque, querido dragón? IV. Hillert, Margaret. What's in the pond, dear dragon? Spanish. V. Title. VI. Title: What's in the pond, dear dragon?
  PZ73.H5572073 2014
  [E]--dc23
                                        2013034965

Manufactured in the United States of America in Brainerd, Minnesota.
240N—012014

Un estanque es una gran cantidad de agua.

A pond is a lot of water.

Aquí crecen lindas flores,
flores amarillas y blancas.

Pretty flowers grow here.
Yellow and white flowers.

Aquí hay algunas que parecen colas de gato.

Here are some that look like cat tails.

¡HUY!
Mira esa tortuga grande en la arena.

WOW!
Look at that big turtle in the sand.

Mira los huevos y los hijitos pequeñitos.
Los hijitos corren hacia el estanque.

Look at the eggs and the little, little babies.
The babies run to the pond.

¿Y qué me dices de esto?   What about this?
Mira esta rana grande.   See this big frog.
La voy a poner en la tierra. I will put it down.

Puede saltar, saltar, saltar.
Lo hace bien.

It can hop, hop, hop.
It is good at that.

Ven aquí ahora.
¡Mira allá abajo!

Come here now.
Look way, way down!

Ay papá, puedo ver algunos peces,
peces grandes y peces pequeños.

Oh Father, I can see some fish.
Big fish and little fish.

Hay uno como el que tenemos en casa.

There is one like we have at home.

Aquí hay algunas hojas para que coma.

Here is something green for it to eat.

¿Quieres comer?
Mamá nos hizo algo de comer.

Do you want to eat?
Mother made something for us to eat.

Ah, sí. Sería una buena idea.
¿Podemos luego jugar a la pelota?

Oh yes. That will be good.
Then can we play ball?

Sí, sí.
Será bueno hacerlo.

Yes, yes.
It will be good to do that.

Aquí va.
Corre para agarrarla.

Here it comes.
Run, run to get it.

Me lastimé la rodilla.

I hurt my knee.

Déjame verla.

Let me see it.

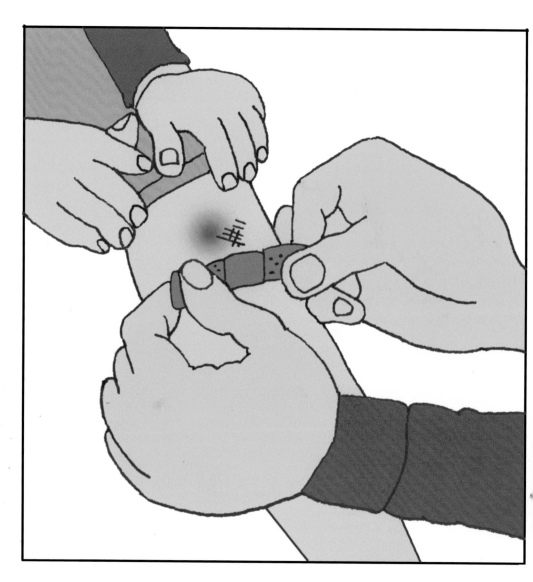

Esto te ayudará.

This will help.

Me siento mejor.
Vamos a ver más cosas.

I feel better.
Let's look for more things.

Papá, mira el botecito rojo.

Look at the little red boat, Father.

Eso es una canoa.

Podemos montarla. Súbete, súbete.

That is a canoe.

We can ride in it. Hop in, hop in.

25

¡Caramba! ¡Qué divertido!
¡Hazla navegar, papá, hazla navegar!

Oh, boy! This is fun.
Make it go Father, make it go!

Ahora estamos en el estanque.
Yo estoy contigo.

Now we are in the pond.
Here I am with you.

Y tú estás conmigo.
¡Ay, qué divertido, querido dragón!

And here you are with me.
Oh what fun, Dear Dragon.

The following activities support the findings of the National Reading Panel that determined the most effective components for reading instruction are: Phonemic Awareness, Phonics, Vocabulary, Fluency, and Text Comprehension.

Phonemic Awareness: The /p/ sound

Substitution: Ask your child to say the following words without the /p/sound:

pat - /p/ = at	pop - /p/ = op	Pam - /p/ = am
pit - /p/ = it	peel - /p/ = eel	pant - /p/ = ant
pair - /p/ = air	pin - /p/ = in	

Phonics: The letter Nn

1. Demonstrate how to form the letters **N** and **n** for your child.

2. Have your child practice writing **N** and **n** at least three times each.

3. Ask your child to point to the words in the book that have the letter **n**.

4. Write down the following words and ask your child to circle the letter **n** in each word:

and	fun	can	down	now
then	something	want	one	canoe
pond	sand	run	green	noon
run	nut			

Vocabulary: Animal Names

1. Ask your child to name the animals in the story. Write the words on separate pieces of paper.

   Turtle   Frog   Fish

2. Read each word to your child and ask your child to repeat it.

3. Mix the words up. Point to a word and ask your child to read it. Provide clues if your child needs them.

4. Mix the words up again. Read the following sentences to your child. Ask your child to point to the word described in the sentence:

   • Name the animal in the story that was in the sand. (turtle)

   • Which animal in the story is one you could have as a pet living in your house? (fish, frog, or turtle)

   • What animal hops? (frog)

Fluency: Echo Reading

1. Reread the story to your child at least two more times while your child tracks the print by running a finger under the words as they are read. Ask your child to read the words he or she knows with you.

2. Reread the story, stopping after each sentence or page to allow your child to read (echo) what you have read. Repeat echo reading and let your child take the lead.

Text Comprehension: Discussion Time

1. Ask your child to retell the sequence of events in the story.

2. To check comprehension, ask your child the following questions:

   • What did they find in the pond?

   • What is the little red boat called?

   • What kind of things do the boy and Father do at the pond?

   • In the story, fish eat plants. What is your favorite thing to eat?

Margaret Hillert ha escrito más de 80 libros para niños que están aprendiendo a leer. Sus libros han sido traducidos a muchos idiomas y han sido leídos por más de un millón de niños de todo el mundo. De niña, Margaret empezó escribiendo poesía y más adelante siguió escribiendo para niños y adultos. Durante 34 años, fue maestra de primer grado. Ya se retiró, y ahora vive en Michigan donde le gusta escribir, dar paseos matinales y cuidar a sus tres gatos.

Photograph by Glenna Washburn

ABOUT THE AUTHOR Margaret Hillert has written over 80 books for children who are just learning to read. Her books have been translated into many different languages and over a million children throughout the world have read her books. She first started writing poetry as a child and has continued to write for children and adults throughout her life. A first grade teacher for 34 years, Margaret is now retired from teaching and lives in Michigan where she likes to write, take walks in the morning, and care for her three cats.

ACERCA DEL ILUSTRADOR David Schimmell fue bombero durante 23 años, al cabo de los cuales guardó las botas y el casco y se dedicó a trabajar como ilustrador. David ha creado las ilustraciones para la nueva serie de Querido dragón, así como para muchos otros libros. David nació y se crió en Evansville, Indiana, donde aún vive con su esposa, dos hijos, un nieto y dos nietas.

ABOUT THE ILLUSTRATOR David Schimmell served as a professional firefighter for 23 years before hanging up his boots and helmet to devote himself to work as an illustrator. David has happily created the illustrations for the New Dear Dragon books as well as many other books throughout his career. Born and raised in Evansville, Indiana, he lives there today with his wife, two sons, a grandson and two granddaughters.